Library of Congress Cataloging in Publication Data

Ambrus, Victor G.
A country wedding.

SUMMARY: Disguised in trousers and hat, a wolf and fox pass themselves off as guests at a wedding party in hopes of a meal.

"An Addisonian Press book."
I. Title.
PZ7.A496Co4 [E] 74-8814
ISBN 0-201-00197-7

ISBN: 0-201-00197-7   LCN: 74-8814

First Printing

A Country Wedding

VICTOR G. AMBRUS

An Addisonian Press book

Addison-Wesley

One day, Bandi the Wolf and Zoli the Fox
heard two old women gossiping about a
wedding that was to be held in the village.
Bandi and Zoli thought greedily about
all the food and wine that would be
given the guests. And they decided
to invite themselves.

Zoli and Bandi stole two pairs of trousers
from a wash-line and a hat from a scarecrow.

They had trouble putting on the trousers as there was no room for their tails. Zoli suggested that they cut holes in the seat of the trousers.

"A very foxy idea," approved Bandi, who had picked a beautiful thistle for the Bride.

When they heard the music begin, Bandi and Zoli
took their places at the end of the
wedding procession.
They danced all the way to the church –
growing hungrier and hungrier.

After the ceremony, they posed for photographs
and kissed the Bride. But all the time
they were waiting for the chance to break into the
kitchen, where all the food was piled up.

When the other guests were not looking, they
slipped away. The first thing they did was to
drink a toast, politely, to the Bride and Bridegroom.

Then they ate all the ice cream and all the cakes,
and perhaps a chicken or two.

Bandi and Zoli drank a few more toasts to the Bride
and sang a song about Love.

At last, Zoli the Fox jumped through
the window and went to sleep in a haystack.
But Bandi was too happy and too fat to move.

So Bandi was caught,
fast asleep!
He jumped into a hole
but got stuck, and
took a terrible beating
before he escaped.
His howls woke Zoli
in the haystack.

The Wolf was so sore all over that he asked the Fox
to carry him home on his back.
But Zoli, who was covered with straw, said,
"Can't you see all my bones sticking out?
If you were a real friend, you would carry *me* instead!"

So Bandi did,
until he heard Zoli singing,
"The Stupid Wolf
carries the Clever Fox –
Oh, what a lovely ride!"
When Bandi heard this,
he threw Zoli to the ground,
and gave *him* a beating.

They were still fighting when the wedding guests
caught up with them. The Bride's Father said,
with a wink to his guests,

"As you are so smartly dressed in *my* trousers,
you had both better come and join the party!"

With that, he stuck a bunch of flowers
behind Bandi's ear, and Bandi and Zoli
had to start singing and dancing straightaway.

The Bride's Mother baked more food,
and the guests had a feast after all –
and a great deal of fun besides!

It was a fine wedding! It went on and on –
day and night – for *five days!*
All the guests thoroughly enjoyed themselves,
except for Bandi the Wolf and Zoli the Fox,
who decided to give up singing and dancing
and weddings *forever!*

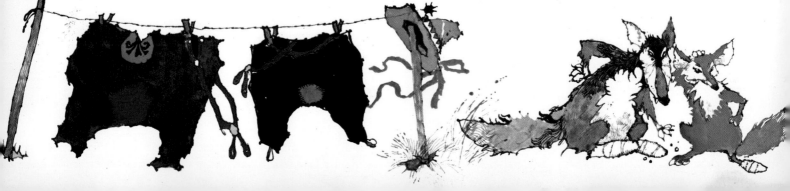